to:
Kelly, Charlotte, Jessica, Jo & Sam.

© 1990 Lorna Turpin
Published by Child's Play (International) Ltd.
Swindon, England.
ISBN 0–85953–511–8 (hard cover)
ISBN 0–85953–512–6 (soft cover)
Printed in Singapore

THE SULTAN'S SNAKES

written and illustrated
by Lorna Turpin

Child's Play (International) Ltd
Swindon   Bologna   New York

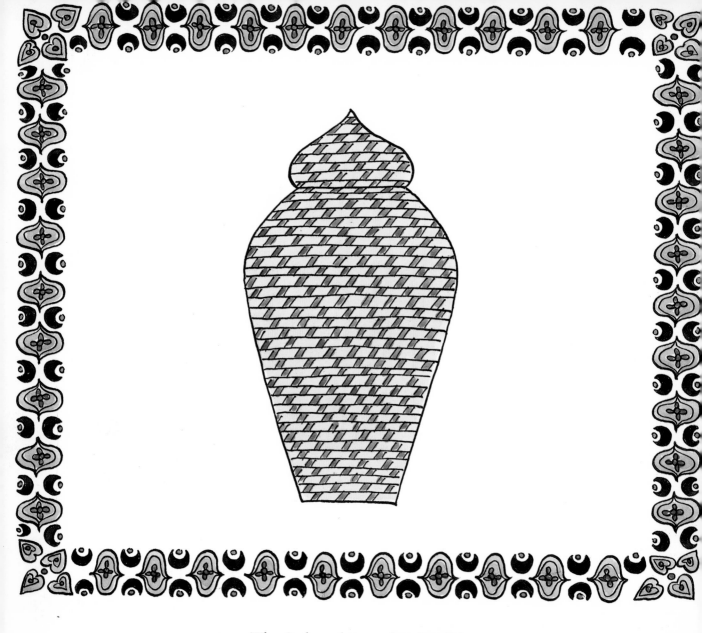

The Sultan kept a basketful
of snakes in his palace.

Every evening, they would entertain his guests
by dancing to the snake charmer's music.

But during the daytime, when they were kept
in the basket, they became very bored.

So they decided to play a trick
on the Sultan.

When he came to wish them good morning,
he found the basket empty.

That's very odd, he thought.
I wonder where they can be.

The Sultan decided that,
as soon as he had finished his breakfast,
he would search the palace.

First, he looked in his lounge,
but he couldn't see any snakes there.

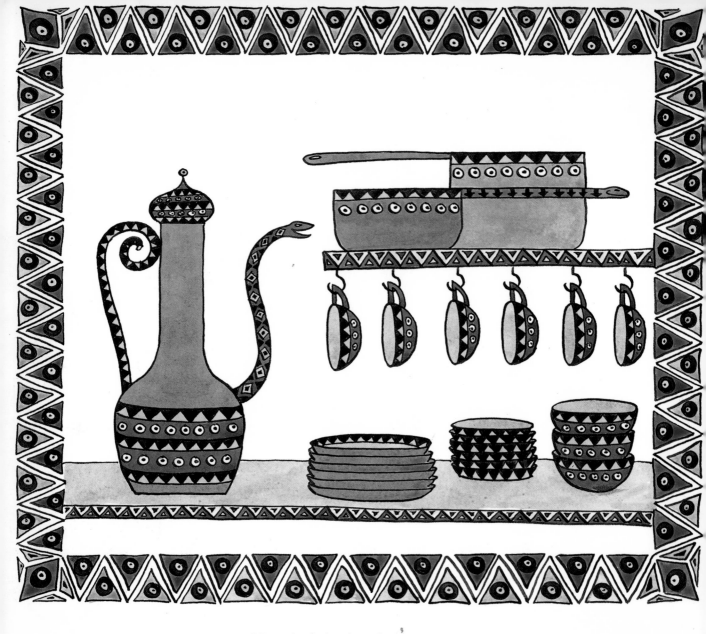

He tried the kitchen.
But there was still no sign.

He couldn't find any
in the bedroom, either.

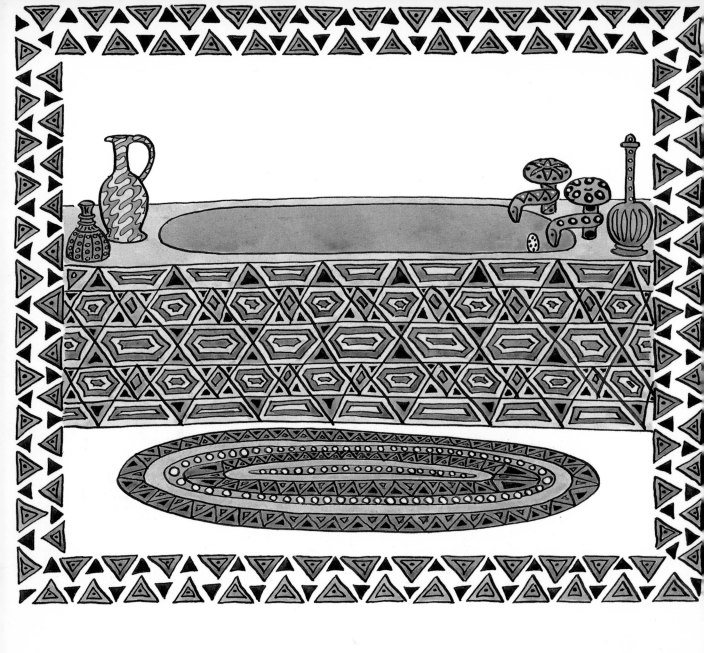

Or the bathroom.

"I'll see if they're in the garden,"
he said.

He searched all over the garden,
but couldn't see a single snake.

So, he asked his wife.

"I haven't seen your snakes," she said.
"Why don't you look after your things properly?"

The guards of the palace
were always on the look-out,
but they hadn't seen any snakes.

So, the Sultan asked the cleaner,
but she hadn't seen them either.

Neither had the cat.

Nor the goldfish.

"This is very strange," the Sultan thought aloud.
"I've searched everywhere and I've asked everyone, but I still can't find them.
I'll just look once more in the basket."

The snakes heard him and hurried back.

When the Sultan opened the basket,
there they were.

"Either my old eyes are playing tricks – or you are," said the Sultan. "I'll never let you out of my sight again."

"We'll see!" smiled the snakes.